LADYBIRD BOOKS, INC.
Lewiston, Maine 04240 U.S.A.
© LADYBIRD BOOKS LTD MCMLXXXVII
Loughborough, Leicestershire, England

Printed in England

The Ugly Duckling

written by RONNE RANDALL
illustrated by ROGER LANGTON

Ladybird Books

It was a warm, sunny day. A mother duck sat on her nest at the edge of a pond, waiting for her eggs to hatch.

One by one, the eggs began to crack open.

''Peep, peep,'' said each little yellow duckling as it poked out its head and looked around.

''Quack, quack,'' said the mother duck, feeling very pleased with herself.

The biggest egg hatched last of all. But the duckling that poked out his head was not little and yellow like the others. He was big and gray and ugly.

"Quack!" said the mother duck. "You are the ugliest duckling I have ever seen!"

The mother duck led her ducklings into the water.

The other ducks gathered around. ''What lovely children you have,'' they told her.

But when they saw the big gray duckling,
they began to laugh. "*That* one isn't lovely,"
they said. "What an ugly duckling he is!"

The mother duck took her ducklings to the farmyard. When the other animals saw the big gray duckling, they all began to shout.

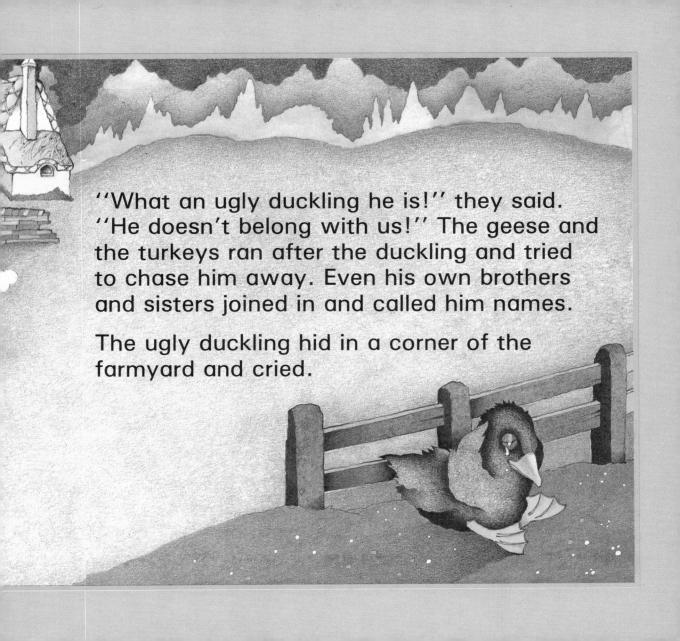

"What an ugly duckling he is!" they said.
"He doesn't belong with us!" The geese and
the turkeys ran after the duckling and tried
to chase him away. Even his own brothers
and sisters joined in and called him names.

The ugly duckling hid in a corner of the
farmyard and cried.

The next morning, the ugly duckling decided to run away.

''I will find a place where no one will make fun of me,'' he said to himself.

He left the farmyard and ran to the great marsh, where the wild ducks lived.

''Perhaps *they* will be kind to me,'' he said sadly.

But the wild ducks were not kind.

"You are very ugly," they said. "You are certainly *not* one of us." And the wild ducks laughed at the duckling.

So the ugly duckling left the marsh.

The wind was blowing, and it was cold. Winter was coming. The ugly duckling was very tired. He had to find a place to stay where he would be warm and safe.

One evening, he came to a little cottage.
The door was open and he went inside.

An old woman lived in the cottage, with a
fat black cat and a plump brown hen.

The old woman didn't mind the ugly duckling, but the cat and the hen wanted him to leave.

"Can you purr?" asked the cat.

"No," said the ugly duckling.

"Can you lay eggs?" asked the hen.

"No," said the ugly duckling.

"Then you must go!" said the cat and the hen.

They chased the ugly duckling out of the cottage and would not let him in again.

The ugly duckling wandered through the countryside for many days. No one would give him a home. No one would be his friend.

All the birds and animals said that he was ugly. He grew more and more sad and more and more tired.

At last he stopped to rest by a lake that was covered with ice. He stayed there all winter, hidden in the reeds. He was cold and hungry and very lonely.

One bright morning in early spring, when all the ice had melted, a flock of beautiful birds came to the ugly duckling's lake.

They had gleaming white feathers and long, graceful necks.

The ugly duckling watched them from his hiding place in the reeds.

"They are the most beautiful birds I have ever seen," he thought. "If only I could be like them!"

The beautiful birds saw the ugly duckling.
The biggest one came over to him.

The ugly duckling tried to hide. He was sure that the bird would make fun of him or try to chase him away.

But the lovely white bird said, ''What a fine young swan you are! You shouldn't be here all by yourself.''

The ugly duckling could not believe what he had heard.

He looked at his reflection in the water. It was true! His feathers were white and gleaming. His neck was long and graceful. He had grown into a handsome swan.

"Come with us!" said the swan.

The ugly duckling spread his wings and rose into the sky. "I never dreamed that I could be so happy," he said, and he flew off proudly with his new friends.